Little Lek Longtail Learns to Sleep
Text © 2016 Bettie Killion
Illustrations © 2016 Beatriz Vidal

Wisdom Tales is an imprint of World Wisdom, Inc.

Library of Congress Cataloging-in-Publication Data

Names: Killion, Bette, author | Vidal, Beatriz, illustrator.
Title: Little Lek Longtail learns to sleep / by Bette Killion ; illustrated
by Beatriz Vidal.
Description: Bloomington, Indiana : Wisdom Tales, [2016] | Summary: In a
Thailand rainforest, a young Argus pheasant uses his long, brightly
colored tail to help conquer his bedtime fears. Includes facts about the
Argus pheasant, an unusual bird that lives in Southeast Asia.
Identifiers: LCCN 2016023612 (print) | LCCN 2016036191 (ebook) | ISBN
9781937786632 (casebound : alk. paper) | ISBN 9781937786649 (epub)
Subjects: | CYAC: Great Argus (Bird)--Fiction. | Bedtime--Fiction. | Fear of
the dark--Fiction. | Self-reliance--Fiction. | Rain forests--Fiction.
Classification: LCC PZ7.K5576 Li 2016 (print)
| LCC PZ7.K5576 (ebook) | DDC
[E]--dc23
LC record available at https://lccn.loc.gov/2016023612

Printed in China on acid-free paper.

Production Date: August 2016,
Plant & Location: Printed by 1010 Printing International Ltd,
Job/Batch #: TT16070417

For information address Wisdom Tales,
P.O. Box 2682, Bloomington, Indiana 47402-2682
www.wisdomtalespress.com

Little Lek Longtail Learns to Sleep

By Bette Killion

Illustrated by
Beatriz Vidal

Wisdom Tales

Years ago in a rainforest in Thailand, an Argus Pheasant hatched from a large speckled egg.

He was a beautiful bird with an unusually long and brightly colored tail. It was the longest and most colorful of any pheasant! His proud mother named him "Little Lek Longtail."

As Lek grew, his tail grew
longer, brighter,
and more beautiful.
Lek was proud of his tail.
He strutted about
the forest, sailing it out
behind him. The other
animals all watched him
in awe.

When he walked among the forest creatures he was so kind and thoughtful that everyone loved him. He made friends with all the other birds—the kingfishers, parakeets, and blue-backed broadbills.

But there were
fierce striped tigers
and black panthers
prowling in the night.
Lek was afraid!

Sometimes at night Lek refused to sleep. "What if a tiger or a panther creeps up our tree?" he would cry. "If I am asleep I will not hear them in time to escape!" His mother would try to comfort him. She held Lek close and sang soft lullabies to him. Lek knew his mother was wise and kind, but still he was afraid.

In the daylight hours Lek walked along the forest paths. He looked at the flying squirrels, lizards, and butterflies. Everyone but Lek seemed happy and protected! One day Lek came down to the river bank. He hid himself and watched the sharp-toothed crocodiles dozing in the sun. They seemed peaceful. Yet, they were ready to dive into the water at any moment.

Down through the yang and mangrove trees came a man and a boy. They both were carrying a large bag. Lek pulled his tail close about him so he could not be seen. He guessed the man and the boy had been out gathering fruit. Now they were on their way home.

They came to a narrow spot in the river. It was filled with the waiting crocodiles. Lek wondered how they would cross. The man pulled out a string of small firecrackers. He lit them and threw them into the river. Lek saw bright, flashing lights and heard loud, bursting sounds.

It frightened him so much he could not move. But the crocodiles did! They scattered as far and as fast as they could swim. Their big mouths were closed and their eyes wide in surprise. The boy and his father then quickly crossed the river.

"Aha!" Lek said to himself. "There is always a way if one just thinks of it." He began to watch the other creatures in the forest. He noticed how they too used their talents to help themselves. So Lek sat down and thought and thought. Suddenly he smiled.

When night came Lek surprised his mother.
He didn't fuss and he didn't cry. He just
crept up along his very own branch and fell
right asleep.

This is the reason. Lek slept with his head on
the tip of the branch. His long, beautiful tail
was spread out behind him. Lek knew
that anything creeping up the tree would
first touch his tail. And because his tail was
so-o-o-o long, he would have time to fly away
to safety. So Lek slept well all night through.

"It is my tail alarm," Lek explained. "What a
wonderful idea!" his mother said.

To this day, Argus
Pheasants in the
forests of Thailand
grow long, beautiful tails.
(Even if they are not so
colorful as Little Lek's.)
When they sleep, they
spread their tails behind
them. With their tail
alarms they rest well
and are never, ever afraid!

Appendix

☙ The Argus pheasant is among the world's most unusual and distinctive birds. The male Argus pheasant is one of the largest of all pheasants and features spectacular wing and tail feathers measuring over three feet long!

☙ The Argus pheasant generally measures 60–80 inches in total length, including a tail of 40–55 inches, and weighs 4.5–6.0 pounds.

☙ The Argus pheasant roosts at night in trees and by day forages on the forest floor. It feeds on a variety of flowers, seeds, fruits, buds, and insects (invertebrates).

☙ The scientific name of the Great Argus is *Argusianus argus*, given by Carl Linnaeus. In Greek mythology, Argus is a hundred-eyed giant, and the Argus pheasant has patterns on its wings that look like eyes (*ocelli*).

⮡ Little Lek is unusually colorful for an Argus pheasant, which is normally not as colorful as other pheasants. The last painting in the book is more representative of a classic Argus pheasant.

⮡ The Argus pheasant normally mates for life (is monogamous).

⮡ The general habitat for an Argus pheasant is in tall, dry, forests, at elevations starting at sea-level and going up to 4,200 feet, but generally below 3,000 feet.

⮡ Sadly, the Argus pheasant is threatened by habitat loss, hunting, and trapping for the cage-bird industry. Due to its population reduction, it is classified as "near threatened."

⮡ The Argus pheasant lives in lowland areas of the biogeographical region of Southeastern Asia know as Sundaland. This region includes parts of Borneo, Indonesia, Malaysia, Myanmar, and Thailand.